Annie Hundley

Tom Hundley

The Drummer Boy

Annie Hundley

Tom Hundley
The Drummer Boy

ISBN/EAN: 9783337376994

Printed in Europe, USA, Canada, Australia, Japan

Cover: Foto ©Andreas Hilbeck / pixelio.de

More available books at **www.hansebooks.com**

TOM HUNDLEY

The Drummer Boy

. OR .

A Secret that General Grant Kept

A DRAMA OF 1861

By Mrs. Annie Hundley

PUBLISHED BY THE AUTHOR

OAKLAND, CALIFORNIA

1899

Tom Hundley

THE DRUMMER BOY

. OR .

A Secret that General Grant Kept

A DRAMA OF 1861

DRAMATIS PERSONÆ

Gen. U. S. Grant.

Officers and soldiers.

Mr. Jeremiah Hundley, father to Annie Hundley (Tom Hundley).

Tom Hundley.

Archibald, James, Richard, and Jesse, brothers to Tom.

Two go off with Southern soldiers.

Joe Dalton, an old friend of Mr. Hundley.

Lieut. Devoe, a friend of Tom Hundley.

Rose Thorn, a young lady.

Mrs. Myers, a friend.

Boat hands, citizens, etc.

ACT I.

Scene 1.

(In Kentucky.) Old Kentucky home; farm-house; stable and barn.

Soldiers on the march; they burn the Hundley homestead and take Mr. Hundley and Tom with them.

(A room in a country house.)

An old-fashioned house and furniture with plenty and comfort, but all in confusion. A large old-time fire-place; a bed of coals, over which hangs an iron pot suspended from a hook; something savory cooking for dinner; a bright-eyed girl plays with her kitten, tossing a ball of yarn, while she laughs with glee.

An old settee; a corner cupboard, with old-fashioned china, some of which came down as treasured relics from ancestors, who fought and bled at Valley Forge; guns on racks supported by deers' antlers; home-made carpets; fine buffalo and Angora goat-skins covering the floor; bees hummed and sipped their nectar from the honeysuckle and wild clematis that crept over the porch, making a very attractive picture of country life. Suddenly a shadow falls on the sunlight that streams in the open door; the girl looks up to see her father; a strange feeling steals over her and checks the merry laugh that bubbles to her lips, as she notes the wild, haggard look in his face; he looked years older than when he parted from her that morning to look after his stock.

Mr. Hundley.—Ah, Annie, my little motherless girl, I have great news for you; the war is brought to our very door; this morning when I kissed you good-by you were asleep in your little bed, the smile of innocence on your sweet lips. I found my barn and storehouses broken open, my goods all gone, my stock driven off, and my farm hands gone. In fact, dear child, we are here alone with nothing left but this house and the contents of that pot that hangs in the fireplace.

(Mr. Hundley walks to the door and looks out.) Exclaims: "They come, they come; the soldiers will soon be here; I see the bayonets gleam as they rise that hill by the old mill.

(Annie clings closer to her father, cries and begs him not to leave her.)

Annie.—O papa! papa! you will not go with the soldiers and leave your little girl; your own little girl!

Mr. Hundley.—No, no, my precious child. When your brothers left us to join the Southern Army, your mother grieved night and day, until, at last, she sickened and died of a broken heart. I promised her on her death-bed never to leave you with strangers, but always to keep you with me. I will keep my word with her. You shall go with me or we will die together. Annie, before they shall separate us I will send your pure spirit to join your sainted mother and I will follow. Is it not better than to leave you alone—for what? (He puts his hand on Annie's head, looks fervently up, saying) O my God, help me now; I can not leave my child with no one to care for her! Is it not better to send her spirit pure and unsullied to that rest in heaven than to leave her to a fate too terrible to think of? Am I going mad? Annie, tell me, child, are you willing to die?

(He walks the floor showing great excite-ment.)

Annie.—Papa, I would rather die than have you leave me.

Mr. Hundley.—Quick, quick, Annie, a thought comes to me; run and change your clothes; put on your brother's coat and pants, and remember you are, after this, my little boy, "Tom Hundley."

Scene 2.

(Soldiers are seen approaching. Annie appears in boy's attire.)

Mr. Hundley.—Bravo! you make a fine boy, Tom; do not forget to play your part; always remember that you are "Tom Hundley," papa's little boy, and we will go together.

(Soldiers approach. Mr. Hundley takes Tom by the hand, goes to meet them.)

A Soldier.—Hello! Who is here? Any more of you?

Mr. Hundley.—Only my little boy, Tom, and I.

Soldier.—What flag do you fly?

Mr. Hundley.—Union flag.

Soldier.—That suits us well; we want just such men as you are in our ranks. (Eyes the tall, well-built man, who stands resolute and fearless before them, for Mr. Hundley feared nothing but leaving his little girl.)

(Soldier looks at Tom, who shyly clings to his father's hand.)

Soldier.—What have you here?

Mr. Hundley.—My little motherless boy.

(Tom shrinks from the soldier—clings closer to his father.)

Soldier.—Come, we must be off; there is

nothing to invite a stay in these regions; the bushes are full of Johnnies, and we are likely to have trouble. Come along, no time to lose.

Mr. Hundley (resolutely).—I am willing to accompany you if you will permit me to take my boy. If you do not take Tom and I alive, you will not care to take us dead. (Stoops over and whispers to Tom.)

Tom.—I am not afraid, papa; we'll live or die together.

(Soldier hears Tom's remark, suspiciously.)

Soldier.—What's that? What's that?

Mr. Hundley.—It means simply this: that if you want to fill your ranks, you can have two, by taking Tom and his father along; if you do not take Tom, you can walk over our dead bodies; but that will not be to your credit.

Soldier.—What will we do with the youngster? How old is he?

Mr. Hundley.—He is just ten years old.

Soldier.—He looks like a little girl, small of his age; if he was a little older we would make a drummer of him; our drummer boy was killed in a skirmish, and we are in need of one.

Tom.—Never mind my size; I can drum as

well as a large boy. I can climb hills and walk all day.

(Soldier looks admiringly at the pretty child, his large, dark eyes all aglow, his wavy hair in curly rings around a brow that denotes intelligence beyond his years.)

Soldier.—Well, well, we can't talk here all day. Come along, come along, Tom, we'll see how you can drum.

(Drum lies on the ground, the kitten plays with the tassel.)

Tom (joyfully).—We'll go, papa, we'll go. (Stoops and picks the kitten up.) Can I take kitty with me, papa?

Mr. Hundley.—No, my child, you will play with guns now.

Tom.—I'll beat the drum. (Picks up the drum, and, to the surprise of the soldiers, beats like an old drummer.)

Soldiers.—That is fine. Tom shall be our drummer boy. Where did you learn to drum?

Tom (simply).—My brothers taught me; I drummed for them when we played soldier.

(Tom takes his father's hand, and they march off.)

ACT II.

Scene 1.

(Camp in woods near Nashville.) It is two years since Tom Hundley left home to join the soldiers. A smouldering camp-fire; soldiers are seen lounging and sitting around. Near the fire on a fallen log sits Tom; his drum is on the ground by his side; his fatigue cap lies on the drum.

These years have developed Tom into rather a delicate-looking but handsome boy; his curly brown hair, fine dark eyes, full of intelligence, attract attention at once; there is something about Tom that wins all hearts; he reclines as if tired—a crimson sash around his shoulders, his drum by his side, a tin cup in his hand—making a pretty picture.

(Two young officers, sitting at a short distance, are looking at Tom.)

Sergeant (who has recently joined the command.)—Say, lieutenant, where did that little chap come from? He looks like he came out of a picture-book; and yet, the men tell me, he has been in a great many hard-fought battles, and is not afraid of anything.

Lieutenant Devoe.—Yes, that boy has a history that old soldiers might envy. You see that tall, fine-looking fellow talking to

Colonel C.? That is the boy's father. Their history is one of interest; it is one illustrating this civil war. The father, it seems, is a northern man. He fell in love with a southern heiress, a beautiful and lovely lady. He made his home in Kentucky, where she had a large property. In the breaking out of the war, two of her sons went off without making their intentions known and joined the southern army. The mother died. The other boys were away somewhere, when, first one side and then the other, raided that part of the country. One day the Hundley home was invaded. Tom with his father joined a raiding party who happened to pass by his farm. I was one of the party. I was quite young myself, only eighteen.

Fear seems to be left out of Tom's composition; he is afraid of only one thing, that is, losing sight of his father for one minute. I never saw anything like their devotion.

I will tell you about their leaving home, and those first days over the hills, rocks, and mud. Tom trudged silently by the side of his father. Not one word could you get out of the youngster but "Yes sir" and "No sir." Tom is no cry-baby. I have only seen him in tears once: that was just as we reached the top of the hill by the old mill, as we retraced our steps. We went a little out of our way to get this man, knowing that he was a Union sympathizer and could give us much needed information about that part of the country. We found that his place had been raided the day before and completely broken up.

The soldiers made a habit of burning the barns when they left. Some stayed behind, setting fire to some rubbish. Soon the whole place was in a blaze.

As we reached the hill-top Tom turned to take a last look; with a piercing scream he threw himself into his father's arms and hid his face.

Against the evening sky (it was almost night) a lurid flame shot up, the roof fell in that sheltered them all—where Tom had spent so many happy hours with father, mother, and brothers. This meant heart-sickening desolation.

Tom sobbed and rocked his little body in an agony of grief. Suddenly lifting his head from his father's shoulder, with brimming eyes, he looked over the landscape; twilight gathered, night was closing in fast. That peculiar haze that follows a southern sunset, rested over all, giving a soft beauty and feeling of repose that was in striking contrast to the lurid glare of the fire and the black, dense smoke that covered the ruins as if with a mourning veil.

Veterans who had faced death on many a battle-field brushed away a tear in sympathy with little Tom, who stood with a last lingering look at the old familiar scene, his beautiful dark eyes suffused with tears—an expression of mute agony I will never forget. His childhood seemed to pass out of his life forever. Appealingly he turned to his father, saying, "Come, papa, it is all over."

Mr. Hundley stood by during this trying ordeal, pale and calm; he dared not think of the happy past. It was like a dream, but thoughts of the little boy by his side aroused him. "Come, Tom," said he, taking Tom by the hand, "we must move on. We have each other, Tom. You must be a true little soldier. Walk on; we must be away from here many miles before to-morrow, or we will go up in smoke, too."

On we marched, two days and nights without food or rest, only halting a few minutes at a time, for a brief respite, then on again. To be without food was not so bad, if we had water, but not one drop until the morning of the third day. It had been raining; we lay close to the ground and drank, as well as we could, the water out of the tracks made by some horses that had just gone before. Even this created a sense of uneasiness, for the indications were that some bush-whackers might lay in ambush—a supposition that was correct. We had a benefit the fourth day; the evening of the third day our little famished squad of soldiers met a provision wagon. We obtained enough for a meal, a little bacon, hard-tack, and coffee.

Little Tom gave expression to our feelings. I heard him say, "Papa, this tastes better than honey and buttermilk biscuits." I looked at the youngster, amazed. You would never believe it possible that he could survive such a forced march over rough mountain roads, without rest, food, or water.

The men were so impressed that they ceased to grumble, ashamed to own that Tom was a better soldier than they were; he actually seemed in better spirits and looked fresher than he did the first day.

(Here comes a sudden interruption to the gossip of the young officers. They had not noticed that the sun's rays were fast sinking behind the horizon, and that a superior officer stood partly concealed by the boughs of a tree, listening to their conversation. Clear and sweet rang the notes of a bugle, calling the attention of the men to the fact that they

had still a bugler, although they were in great
perplexity to get a substitute for the one left
dead on the ground where the last battle had
been fought.)

(Note.—These bugle notes were vocal.)

Scene 2.

(Woods.)   General Grant is seen; his horse
is hitched to the bough of a tree.   As the
General approaches them, the young officers
spring to their feet, saluting him.

Gen. Grant.—Who is that ؍ boy that is
drummer, bugler, and soldier, yet looks like
a modest young girl in boy's clothes?

Lieut. Devoe.—I have often thought he
looked like a girl, and yet his name is Tom
Hundley; that tall, handsome man talking to
his colonel is the boy's father.   The little chap
is like his father's shadow.

Gen. Grant.—What was that about his
marching without food or water for two days?
Did you say there was a fight, too?

Lieut. Devoe.—The fourth day we fell in
with bush-whackers.   Whiz, bang—the shot
flew around our heads like hail—a surprise,
as we were in a bit of wood.   The smoke
from the guns blinded us, we were in such
close range.   It was short, but severe.   After
the fight was over, many of our men lay

2

around dead and dying. We hastily dug a trench, buried our dead, and prepared to move on. We missed our little drummer boy. His father was wild; he thought his boy was dead. We soon found him, sitting as if dazed, with a dead man's head in his lap, still holding the flask to his lips.

"Tom, Tom," we called, and looking up, Tom laid the dead man's head gently down, saying, "He groaned and begged for water, and I ran to get him some. He choked and died."   •

"Tom, were you not afraid of the bullets," I asked. "Yes, a little," Tom answered, "but I could not see papa for the smoke. I was more afraid of losing him. The poor man kept begging for water. I had my canteen full and I wanted to give him some. When I looked around I could not see papa. I was afraid I would be left alone with the dead man."

Gen. Grant (his eyes suspiciously moist).— Bring the boy to me. I must speak to him.

(Tom Hundley hastily catches up his drum, swings it across his shoulder, surprised and delighted to at last talk face to face with the great general under whose orders he had marched so often.)

(Tom approaches and salutes.)

Gen. Grant.—You are the boy drummer, bugler, and soldier. Well, you are a brave lad and deserve promotion. I did not have an idea that we had so young a soldier in our service, but you can remember that General Grant is proud of you; you should enlist at once. You shall not be forgotten. Your father will be proud of you some day, my little hero; your country will be proud of you, and your General will not forget you. When this war is over, come to see General Grant, give that bugle call, and he will need no other reminder.

(A tall man stepped forward, saluted the General, and asked for a few words in private.)

(General Grant easily recognized him as Tom's father; the likeness was striking.)

(The lieutenant and Tom walked away, leaving Mr. Hundley in earnest conversation with General Grant.)

Scene 3.

(General Grant and Mr. Hundley. They walk in the edge of the woods.)

Gen. Grant.—Well, I must go; I will not forget to make a note of this; it seems a hard case. You say she has fought her way for two years, walking over the battle-fields with her little feet red with blood, beating the drum without fear. It would now be cruel to part you. It would break her heart to take her away. I'll consider the matter. In the meantime I will order that you are not separated, and General Grant will keep your secret. It is very remarkable. There must be some recognition of your faithful service, and also a suitable reward for your little "Joan of Arc." I now understand why she cast her eyes down and looked so abashed when I suggested that she enlist in the regulars. But she will some day be remembered for her heroism. Seek me out when this war is ended. Honorable mention shall be made, and your little girl provided for. You have the word of General Grant. (Mounting his horse he rode away.)

ACT III.

Scene 1.

(Indiana.) After the war. Soldiers have disbanded. Mr. Hundley and Tom are found on a canal boat owned by an old friend of Mr. Hundley's, Joe Dalton, who has invited them to stay with him until they can find a home.

Tom Hundley has dropped his soldier clothes; appears as Miss Annie Hundley. She is now nearly thirteen, a lovely girl, with promise of a beautiful womanhood, not spoiled by her army experience, but rather more sedate than girls of her age. Her face is full of thought that gives her the appearance of a girl of sixteen, yet lights up with a smile that is very engaging.

Annie is sitting on deck with her father's friend, Joe Dalton, when a cry of "Fire" is heard. All is hurry, bustle, and confusion. There is a loud report, a crashing of timbers, cries and shouts. Annie feels a sudden shock, is thrown in the water, loses consciousness.

Scene 2.

Private residence. Annie Hundley is taken to a beautiful house surrounded by fine grounds, every appearance of wealth; she is cared for by kind friends, recovering from a long illness. She is at last out for a stroll in the grounds, finds a seat in an arbor overgrown with roses; a little tired, she pensively rests her head on a mossy rock and falls asleep; starting suddenly up she cries aloud, "To arms! to arms!" then throwing her head back she makes the bugle notes, sweet and

clear. She shades her eyes with her hand
and murmurs softly, "Was it a dream? I
saw General Grant on a large chestnut horse;
he dropped a sable plume; I picked it up,
and—" she started with surprise, for, sitting
close by, looking at her intently, she saw a
young officer, whose face seemed strangely
familiar.

The young officer speaks.

Officer.—Can this be Tom Hundley's sister? I am Colonel Devoe. I knew a little
drummer boy by that name when I was in
camp near Nashville, during the civil war.
Tell me, please, are you his sister?

(Annie, blushing crimson, appeared em-
barrassed, then, with one of her rare smiles,
threw her head back, and again made those
bugle notes; smiling at his puzzled look,
she said) "Colonel Devoe, do you know me
now?"

Col. Devoe.—Can it be Tom Hundley?
(Stammers in confusion) Were you really a
girl?

(Annie hides her face in her hands. She
knows now that she loves the brave young
officer. She tries to hide the secret from
him, for she does not yet know if her love is
returned.)

Col. Devoe.—Those friends who found you

lying on the bank are my cousins, Annie.
They found you after the explosion, stunned
and almost dead. You were picked up by
some boatmen who saw you as you were
thrown in the water; you were carried up to
the residence of my cousin, Mrs. St. Claire.
I came on a visit, little dreaming that I would
find "Tom Hundley."

Annie (blushing).—Do not call me "Tom,"
or ever allude to my army experience, please,
Colonel Devoe. Your friends could not understand it as you do. I am afraid they
would think me bold. I do so dread the
criticism of society people. Your cousins
have been so kind, in fact, they have made a
perfect pet of me; I have been so happy.
You will see what a difference it will make
as soon as they find I have been thrown on
the mercy of the world—a poor, motherless
child. The coldness will grow over them; I
can't tell how, but I know I will feel it; and
I shrink from the trying ordeal of meeting
with polite snubs and cold looks from my
sister-women more than I did from all the
bullets that whizzed around my head when I
was a little drummer boy in the army.

Col. Devoe.—Annie, my heart aches to
think that so soon you begin to feel the coldness of the world. Sit down on this mossy

rock, and let me talk with you and look at
you, my little comrade! Tom, my dear little friend; how often I have thought of you!
I will tell you some time.

(They sit down, Lieutenant Devoe holding
Annie's hand.)

Lieut. Devoe.—Annie, can it be possible
that this tall, beautiful young lady is really
the pretty, curly-headed little drummer boy
who ran to keep up with his father, beating
the drum in the thickest of the fight; and
when the battle ended, bending over the
wounded and dying, with the face of a little
angel, and hands that were ever ready to give
water from the little canteen that hung from
his shoulder, full of crystal drops that meant
more to the poor wounded soldier than all
the hoarded treasures of the Rothschilds?
Annie, you are the bravest girl I ever saw.
Did you realize your danger when in the
thickest of the fight, with the bullets flying
like hail around you, the smoke of battle almost hiding you from sight, and only the
sound of your drum to guide us on to the
front?

Little fairy! think for a moment and tell
me, is your life charmed? The men grew
superstitious and followed your drum as rev-
erently as they did the colors.

(Colonel Devoe, his eyes looking into Annie's with an expression that filled her with happiness, and his words giving her the assurance that she was not forgotten.)

(At last Annie found voice to answer him.)

Annie.—Colonel Devoe, allow me to express my appreciation of all your kindness to me in those weary marches. How many acts of thoughtful care relieved me of many hardships! After all these years do you indeed remember me?

Col. Devoe.—Do I remember you, little one? Does one forget the sunshine and flowers that brighten one's life? I am glad to find you here, Annie, at Belleview. We will take rides and walks along the river bank. I will tell you a story that will let you see how well I remember you. You are quite young, Annie, to speak of "years gone by." I suppose the exciting scenes of battlefields and the very unusual experiences you have had, make a full-grown woman of you, when in reality you are only a child in years.

Annie.—I fear I will be missed. I must return to the house and bid my friends adieu; my father is ill, and needs my care. I must now say good-by until we meet again.

(Exit Annie.)

Scene 3.

(House at Belleview. Front door.)

Annie returns to the house; meets Mrs. St. Claire at the door.

Annie.—How can I thank you, kind friend, for all you have done! I owe to you more of happiness than I have had since I was a child in my old Kentucky home. I will take it with me in memory like a sweet dream; but this life is not for me. Some day, if I have the pleasure of meeting you again, I will tell you a story; how a little girl was left motherless, and had to follow the fortunes of her father. But, alas! the world applauds the brave, weaves laurel wreaths for her heroes, but too often slights and blights the lives of those who are just as deserving. Is not the heart's blood of one poor private just as red as that of a great general?

Mrs. St. Claire.—Annie, I am amazed. Is this my gentle little friend? To what do you allude? You talk as if you had a world of experience; the woman's soul speaks from your flashing eyes. Your words would fit one of riper years.

Annie.—Oh! I could tell you things would fill a volume. I tremble and shrink from the cold, hard criticism of the world as I would not from open cannon's mouth! But I must say good-by. Your loving words and gentle care will never be forgotten. I must seek out my friends, and bid you a fond adieu.

Scene 4.

(Drawing-room; guests seated.) They enter the house. Annie starts, with a feeling that causes her heart to beat faster, when she sees among the guests, Colonel Devoe. He is sitting by the side of a beautiful, proud-looking girl, who is fashionably dressed and evidently pleased to absorb his attention.

Mrs. St. Claire.—Annie, let me introduce a friend, Miss Rose Thorn; Miss Hundley, Miss Thorn.

(This was all, and yet it seems years of agony to Annie. She could not define her feelings. There seemed suddenly to rise a great barrier between her and all that meant happiness. This assured ease and grace of manner, the elegant dress, luxurious surroundings of wealth and aristocracy, were in painful contrast to the canal boat, the rough cabin, the open air, the life in camp, where a coarse blanket was a luxury; and yet was not her heart's blood as red as theirs? Did they do more for their country than she. Did they deserve the applause of the world more than she? These thoughts passed like lightning through her brain; she felt dizzy and sick and longed to get out into the open air; even a canal boat would have been a relief.)

Col. Devoe.—Miss Hundley, we were talking of a drive over to the fort. I expect to meet some brother officers, and we will have a dance and return by moonlight. You will go, of course?

Annie.—No, I must decline, for I leave in a few minutes. I have summons to meet my father, who has just found out where I am. He is sick and can not come to me. I bid you all adieu.

(Exit Annie.)

Scene 5.

(A poor room in the suburbs of the city. A sick man lies on a bed, his head bandaged. A young girl is seated near.)

Mr. Hundley.—Annie, I am very sick; I must tell you something I have on my mind. You remember that I have nothing to expect from your mother's estate, such are the fortunes of war. What is to become of you? My brave little girl. I can not bear to think of leaving you alone.

Annie (sobbing as if her heart would break).—Papa, papa, do not talk like this;

you will live; I will get work and help you.
O papa! this world is so cruel, I wish we
were in camp again, you with your gun, and
I with my drum and hard-tack.

Mr. Hundley.—No, Annie, you were a
child then: now you are a woman. Be brave;
do your duty, little one; be not afraid. God
will take care of you. Annie, there is something I must tell you. The world is like a
great battle-field; there must be a controlling
force; there is plotting and tactic that require
a great deal of engineering. A little drummer boy is good in his place, but he could not
meet the contending forces alone. You are
young, Annie, very young. You have
neither home nor mother's care. I think it is
better that you be provided for before I join
the soldiers on the other side. Annie, Joe
Dalton will care for you; he is much older than
you are, but he is all the better able to take
care of you. Joe wants you for his wife. Annie, what is the matter? (For Annie was
crying as if her heart would break.)

Annie.—Never mind, papa, you are sick.
I will nurse you so well that you will soon be
well again. Let Joe Dalton rest, I want only
you.

Mr. Hundley.—I am very sick, Annie, the

sickness of death, I am afraid. Joe Dalton
can make you a home, remember.

ACT IV.

Scene 1.

(A grove of trees.) A girl sits on a fallen
log, her hat is in her lap, as she idly twines
flowers around the brim. The smile that
brightened her face and dispelled the idea of
sadness has faded into a wistful, far-off look,
that is touching in one so young. Annie
does not observe a young man standing a
short distance off, closely observing her every
movement. Restlessly, she pats her feet, and
sings a little song that she learned in camp
life. Suddenly throwing her hat away, she
walks rapidly up and down the little path,
clasping and unclasping her hands. Throwing herself down in a passion of tears, she cries
aloud.

Annie.—Oh, this cruel world! What is
there here for me?—Heartache! Yes, I
could beat my drum to drown the groans that
would burst from my lips; to still the cry of
pain, worse, far worse, than gaping wounds
by shot and shell. These thrusts, sent by

friends, not foes, these heart-cuts, make greater havoc. My father! my father! did you but know the fate that you consigned me to, your spirit would come back to comfort me! But yes, I promised you, and I'll be brave and true.

(She picks up her hat to go, wipes her tears away, throws her head back with a laugh that sounds like the echo of heart-strings breaking; loud and sweet ring the bugle notes.)

(A shadow crosses her path. She looks up to see Colonel Devoe standing before her. He stretches out his arms. In tender accents he calls) "Annie, Annie, my own love! I will try to keep you from every breath of harm. Smile once again! That sweet little spirit that hovered over our weary marches, and kept us always hoping, must not fail now. I am selfish, Annie; I want you away from all the world, to preside over my destiny, like the good fairy you are. Tom, my little comrade! to be remembered when telling our stories around our own fireside, but to the rest of the world will be Annie Devoe if—" (But Annie has fainted. He catches her, kisses her hands and face, runs to the spring that falls out of the rocks near by, gets water, returns to find her reviving, gives her

a drink. She sips the water from a cup that
he takes out of his pocket; then, deadly pale,
with a face full of a great sorrow, she looks at
him, one long, intense, soulful look, that
means a last farewell. She speaks.)

Annie.—Colonel Devoe, when I left you
that fateful day at Belleview, I felt a world of
conflicting emotion. I knew my heart for
the first time, when I saw you seated by
Miss Thorn, she, rich and beautiful; I, only
"Tom, the drummer boy." Do not call it
jealousy; it is fate. A great gulf seemed to
spring up between us. I little dreamed that
you cared for me other than a friend. Listen
patiently until I tell you all. My father was
ill—he who gave me all the care and love of
father and mother both for so many years of
trial and hardship. You know better than I
can tell you. I saw him ill and suffering, his
health completely broken from the long, hard
marches, to say nothing of the hard-fought
battles, the double care he had had to keep
me with him. To gratify his least wish I
would give my life. He agonized at the
thought of leaving me homeless—alone. I
made up my mind to do as he wished. I felt
that my love for you was only another pain.
I did not for an instant dream that you loved
me. (Clasping her hands in despair.) Oh,

what have I lost! What have I done! To please my father,—I—I—I—m-arried Joe Dalton.

(Pale as death, Colonel Devoe stood silent; then with a great effort said) "Annie, there is no blame. Had I but known how you were placed! I have been searching for you everywhere. Only by accident to-day did I find you, only to lose you again. Do your duty, Annie, as you always have done. Sometime, sometime, we'll meet in heaven."

Scene 2.

A small room furnished poorly. A baby cries in its cradle. A rough, ill-favored man, brutalized with drink, walks the floor muttering curses. Suddenly the door opens. A young girl enters, thinly clad, icicles clinging to her garments, a shawl thrown over her head, a dash of snow on shawl, and stray curls that are blown by the winter's blast, escaped from their fastenings, falling about her face, and giving a weird beauty to the features that, although pinched with cold, are young and handsome. The great blue-gray eyes look out from their silken lashes with mingled fear and hatred at the man she calls her husband. Piteously, she turns to the cradle and takes the infant in her arms, caressing him in

3

tender accents, while the snowflakes drop
from her curls on her baby boy's face.
Springing like a tiger from his lair on a poor
little fawn that has strayed in his way, he
grasps her roughly by the arms.

Joe Dalton (with a muttered curse).—Annie, did you bring the liquor (shaking her
roughly)? Answer, or, by heaven, I'll cut
your throat, and make an end of the brat,
too! He's been crying here this hour.

Annie (looking him firmly in the face).—
Joe, you are no man to speak and act like
this. See my frozen dress. It sleets and
snows. I could not get my wages for the
work I did. The men at the tavern were surprised that you would send me out in this
cold, cold sleet for whisky; and—

(With a fierce yell, Joe Dalton caught the
baby, threw it across the room, then deliberately sat down with a chuckle, razor in hand,
to sharpen the edge.)

Annie.—Joe! Joe! is this the way you fulfil
the promise made my father on his death-
bed? Did you not say you would care for
me tenderly all the days of your life? O my
God! Am I going mad? Can I trust my
senses? Joe Dalton, you have murder in
your heart! Look at me now, and have some
pity! I am only a child; I am not yet fifteen.

Life is sweet, although you have made it so
bitter to me that I would say, do your worst,
put me out of my misery, but for my baby's
sake. My boy! my darling baby boy!
(With outstretched arms. Annie caught her
boy from the floor, raining passionate kisses
on his head and face.)

(Joe Dalton, with a mad spring, caught
her head, holding it back, the curls clutched
tight in one hand, while with the other he
raised aloft his razor, was in the act of
bringing it swiftly across her throat, when a
piercing scream from Annie attracted the
attention of a policeman who was passing the
door at that very moment. Rushing in, he
struck the man's arm a heavy blow with his
club, sending the razor flying across the
room. Annie, with her baby clasped in her
arms, fell fainting to the floor.)

Policeman.—Ho, ho, you are a pretty fellow! I'll see if justice can be meted out to
you. A cool night to cut your wife's throat
in. Come along—come along.

(Sullenly Joe Dalton submitted to be hand-
cuffed and followed the officer out.)

(Annie slowly regains consciousness. Lifting herself to her elbow, she gazes around be-
wildered.)

Annie.—Am I dreaming, or did Joe try to

kill me? Where am I? Where am I? Oh,
yes, here is baby! Now it all comes to me.
(Slowly rising from the floor, she picks her
baby up. Seating herself in a low rocker,
she sings a little song. Then, laying him
softly down, she walks up and down the floor.)

Annie.—O papa, papa, come to me now!
If I could only see you once again, 'twould
ease this gnawing pain that eats my heart
away, and I would take courage as of yore,
when battles raged and gory plains were covered with the slain; when sable night her
mantle spread to cover o'er the dead. I'd
cling to you, my father dear, and in your
presence cast off fear; so come at once without delay, to cheer my now benighted way.

(Dimly a shadow is outlined on the wall,
growing plainer, until Annie sees a shadowed
picture of her father. The picture remains a
moment, then fades.)

(Annie stands looking rapturously at the
shadow-like image so softly outlined.)

Annie.—My father! My father! 'Tis well!
'Tis well! I'll comfort take, and courage,
too! I'll go out into the world's great mart,
and, like a sailor, use my chart. I'll find a
harbor safe, and there I'll rest me from the
fury of these storm-crest waves. I'll hie me
to some sunny clime, where birdlets sing and

flowers bloom. I'll leave these shadows and the gloom that haunts my pathway here.
(Knocking is heard at the door. Policeman enters.)

Policeman. — What! Ho! You must away; you dare not stay! Your life is in danger! Not a minute lose! But take your boy and fly! If you but linger here too long, and jail bars break, then you may quake with fear; for soon or late, with fiendish hate, your life he'll take, with curses deep. In guilt so steeped that pity sleeps to wake no more, this man will follow you from shore to shore! Then stay not here, but with your baby fly to some safe spot! There is no reason in this drunken sot. Your pleading is in vain. 'Tis useless to entreat: the man was born without a heart! Now, like a noble woman, go, and play your part. Forget the past. New friends you'll find; and may the angels guide your way.

(Exit policeman.)

(Annie gathers a shawl around her, and, with baby in her arms, goes out into the gathering gloom, meets a lady who takes her home with her.)

Scene 3.

Mrs. Myers' house. Room with three

doors; table; Mrs. Myers standing with a box in her hand, which she places on the table, takes a sponge, dips it in box, then looks at it.

Mrs. M.—Yes, with this I will change her so completely that her villain husband will not know her. Justice! where is justice, when this man with murder in his heart is let loose? (Goes to the window, looks out.) Oh, there he goes, crouching in the shadow of the wall! His gun is loaded. With a deadly aim he means to kill his wife and baby boy! The fiend! He'll not succeed! I'll send them out to pass by him; with speed of engine, steam, and rail, outwit the villain.

(Door opens; reveals a stairway. Annie looks timidly in with her baby in her arms.)

Mrs. M.—Come, Annie, now's your time. Make haste, my child, no time to lose. I can not longer hide you here; the villain's free to follow you; let loose this day. With gun in hand, he goes in every house, demands his wife and child. In terror women sit, and children frightened cry. Make haste to fly! 'Tis the old story of the "Raven and the Dove." Here, I will make a raven of you; for a whiie the color you may wear.

(She takes a sponge and blacks Annie's face. Then Annie holds baby, standing on the table, while Mrs. Myer blacks baby's face.)

(Taking colored handkerchief, she makes a turban on Annie's head, slips a striped skirt over her, puts a plaid shawl around her, slips big hoop earrings over her ears, puts large, coarse shoes on her feet, wraps baby in an old shawl, puts money in Annie's hand.)

Annie.—Dear friend, how can I ever thank you for your more than kindness! In all my trouble people shunned me. They were afraid of the vengeance of my husband. Did they but show me kindness, he swore he would kill the one who gave me shelter. You, with fearless, noble thought, did take me in and hide me well. For three long days and nights my vigil have I kept in attic dark, not daring to move out into the light. My baby's noisy prattle did I stop, for fear 'twould bring him to your door.

Mrs. M.—(Looks out the window.) He comes! He comes! Go by him without fear. Haste to the train. I hear the whistle blow. (Whistle blows.) In Cincinnati you will find a home. Farewell, dear child. May heaven speed you on your way.

(Shoves Annie out the door and closes it.)

(Street scene. Annie outside of door, with her baby clasped tight in her arms. Sees Joe

Dalton coming with gun in hand. She makes a dash to go by him. He turns, points his gun at her a moment, then, with a muttered curse, goes on.

Joe Dalton.—Only a colored girl, her baby in her arms. I thought 'twas her. But I will find her yet, and never rest until I send a bullet through her heart.

(He stands looking at the trigger of his gun.)

(Curtain falls leaving Joe Dalton on the stage. Annie hears car whistle. Goes off at side door.)

ACT V.

Scene 1.

(House in Cincinnati.) Four stories; side window. Child looking out of window. On the street, looking up at the child, stands Annie Hundley. She is now twenty. Her little boy, a little more than five years old, is a prisoner in that room.

Annie.—I have called and no one answers. I have tried the doors, and all are locked. My boy is in that room. I must have him. I left him, as I thought, in careful hands, while I did earn his bread and mine. I will have him! My child! My child! Not iron bolts or bars can keep me out!

(Child at window calls) "Mama, mama, come take me out!"

Annie.--Here is a ladder. (Finds a ladder.) I will climb up to the skies, but I will bring my baby down.

(She starts to climb the ladder, when a hand is laid on hers. Looking up, she sees a friend indeed—Colonel Devoe. Annie clasps her hands and looks at him, then appealingly at the window.)

Col. Devoe.—Annie (he takes both her hands and holds them tightly), I have found you at last, and I will not let you go. Annie, what does all this mean?

Annie.—It means my child's a prisoner in that house, but get him down, and I will answer you.

(Child beats on the window and calls frantically) "Mama, mama, come take me out."

(Springing lightly up the ladder, Colonel Devoe with his fist knocks the window in, and with the little boy in his arms, the child's flaxen curls resting on his shoulders, takes him down and gently places him in Annie's arms, then takes them both in his arms.)

Col. Devoe.—Once more we meet, dear love! I've heard it all. You'll not repeat

the story, of your flight. The villain's dead
who made your life a blight, and turned your
sunshine into darkest night.

Annie.—Is he dead? Joe Dalton dead?
Oh, tell me, am I free! The chains that
bound me in a hateful bondage, are they
broken, too?

Col. Devoe.—Be still, my love. Let not
the memories of the past intrude. 'Tis past;
he's dead. He followed you with murder in
his heart. He found that you had fled, and
followed on your way. To rest, he threw
himself across the track, regardless of a coming train. He slept, nor did he wake in time.
I'll say no more. You're free; you're mine!

(Annie stands with her boy holding her
right hand in both of his, her left hand im-
prisoned by Colonel Devoe.)

The End.

To the Public:

This drama portrays the true life of a little
girl who followed her father into the battle
fields of the civil war of 1861. Her home de-
stroyed, her mother dead, she bravely beat
her drum in many a hard-fought, bloody battle.

Her father died from injuries received in the war. Broken in health, he was taken to a public institution, and died there in want.

His little girl, left at the age of thirteen, was married to the man of her father's selection. This marriage proved a very unhappy one for her. The man was killed at a railroad crossing by a train of cars. She was again free.

Often she thought of the kind words of General Grant, and wished to remind him of his promise, by sounding once more those "bugle notes," but she had no opportunity of seeing him. She was in a far-off town, without means to accomplish her purpose. General Grant passed away to the soldier's rest. She still lives to remember the promise he made and the secret that he kept.

If any one doubts this, let them write to the original little drummer boy, "Tom Hundley," Oakland, Alameda County, California, and they can have corroboration of all these facts.

Poor Tom, with all his love for his country, his adoration for his great general, and his heroism, is still battling with fate.

He can still sound the bugle notes as of yore.

May the spirit of General Grant breathe on

these leaves, fragrant with the life of the brave little girl who met her destiny like a hero.   Yours ever, and

Our Country Forever,

Tom Hundley.

The object in writing this history of my eventful life is not a selfish one. I wish to give all my time and means to build a home for children who are left as my boy was; to spend all my future life in building it up and giving shelter to the friendless ones who are not orphans in the eyes of the law, but are left helpless, drifting with the tide, into whirlpools of vice and wretchedness, with no home or friends. Poor little waifs! God bless and save them. Who will help me? I will search the darkest corners of the streets and alleyways, and bring into the home boys and girls who have mothers left struggling against too great odds to keep their little ones. I will care for the children and try to help the mothers get work; if the fathers are sick, to help them; if the fathers are drunkards, to protect the children, giving them shelter and instruction to make them good men and women. My whole heart is in this work. I shall sell my little book, take the proceeds, and dedicate it to this purpose.

When a kind public will read my life's history, they will understand why I am so interested. I was left an orphan by the death of my father. He died from the result of his sickness contracted in the army, leaving me to the care of the man I married, a child of only thirteen years.

One year later I found I was the child wife of a drunken brute. A beautiful baby was born—a little boy. Among strangers, too young to know what my rights were, I felt very unhappy. Things grew worse. I had to go out begging work. When I did not bring home money he would beat me cruelly. He compelled me to supply him with whisky. In terror, I have taken my baby in my arms, hiding in the shrubbery in the cold rain and sleet, afraid to go in the house. One day when my little boy was one year old, my husband came home, demanded my wages, to satisfy his craving for drink. I refused. He deliberately sharpened his razor, held my head back, and was proceeding to cut my throat, when my frantic screams brought the policeman, who rescued me from his fury, took him off to jail, then advised me to flee to some place where he could not find me. Trembling with fright, my baby clasped in my arms, I rushed across the street and found shelter in the house of Mrs. Myers, a kind

neighbor, who hid me in her garret. Three
days later he came with a gun, looking for
me. He looked in every house, vowing vengeance, declaring he would kill both baby and
me. Imagine my terror, trying to keep my
baby quiet so that his noisy prattle would not
betray my hiding-place.

Mrs. Myers, afraid that he would kill her
as well, procured some blacking, and with
this disguised both baby and me. She also
kindly furnished a little money. With this I
ventured out, passed my irate husband by;
but my change of color so disguised me that
he did not recognize me. I took the train
for Cincinnati. I worked hard to make ex-
penses and keep my darling baby, sometimes
leaving him to the care of others. Often my
boy was treated harshly, locked up all day by
himself, and starved. I would work all day
and wet my pillow with my tears. I would
pray for help, and wonder why a kind provi-
dence would leave me to suffer when I was
doing all I could. I know that if we trust our
all to God He will help us. I feel that I suf-
fered to make me realize the great work
needed to rescue others; but for this bitter experience I would not be willing to give my all
to help the unfortunate; I would not be willing to make ceaseless efforts to build this
home. I hope that others may follow, and

that thousands more will spring up with open doors to take in all children who need protection. Orphan asylums refuse those who are not orphans; the children must suffer for the faults or misfortunes of their parents. This home will be open to all! When I think of the time that I, a child wife, afraid that I might return to find my baby dead, killed by a savage who called himself a man, sent to the tavern to buy whisky with my own hard-earned wages, or pay the penalty—a cruel beating—if I refused! The men at the tavern pitied me; they treated me with respect; it was my own husband who waited to snatch the liquor from my hands without even noticing my dress frozen stiff with ice and snow! Oh! those days of cruel torture!

One day he sat on a railroad crossing; the train that came whirling by freed me from the cruel bondage.

I worked some years, saving up my little earnings, and bought a little home; my son was growing every year and helped me. I met with many misfortunes; finally I drifted to California. In Oakland I bought a home, and cared for little ones who had mothers to love them, but were too poor to provide. I would take the little ones and keep them, to let the mothers go out to work. Oh! what a great good I may do!

The returns from my book, and any and all money, large or small, that may be sent to me for this purpose, will be gratefully received and applied to this home for friendless children. All who kindly respond will be given ample proof of the honesty and sincerity of all concerned.

Hoping to meet with sympathy, and to receive some help from those who love little children, I am, most truly,

Your obedient servant,

ANNIE HUNDLEY.

(Tom Hundley.)

Oakland, Alameda Co., Cal.

This is to certify that Mrs. Annie Hundley is well known and held in highest estimation in this community, especially by the Educational Department, she having letters of high commendation from some of the oldest teachers in the department, substantiating her record for kindness, capability, etc., etc., for giving careful and practical training and a home to friendless children.

ANNIE HUNDLEY GLUD.

Subscribed and sworn to before me this 11th day of November, 1899.

F. C. WATSON,

(Seal) Notary Public.